Collected Prose

PAUL CELAN

Collected Prose

TRANSLATED FROM THE GERMAN
BY ROSMARIE WALDROP

The Sheep Meadow Press
Riverdale-on-Hudson
New York

These selections originally appeared in the German language in *Gesammelte Werke,* edited by Beda Allemann and Klaus Reichert (Frankfurt: Suhrkamp, 1983), vols III, V.

All inquiries and permission requests should be addressed to:
> The Sheep Meadow Press
> P. O. Box 1345
> Riverdale-on-Hudson, NY 10471

Distributed by:
> Consortium Book Sales and Distribution, Inc.
> 287 East 6th Street, Suite 365
> St. Paul, MN 55101

Celan, Paul.
> Collected Prose.

Library of Congress Catalog Card Number 90-30112
ISBN 0-935296-92-1

Printed in the United States of America

CONTENTS

INTRODUCTION

Celan's prose writings make a slim volume. For
Celan, whose poems moved ever closer to silence,
prose was too noisy a medium. Not for him, the
'buntes Gerede'. It is indeed fortunate that various
occasions prodded him to write these texts. They
are invaluable for defining the *place* from which
Celan writes.

The text to which Celan himself gives most
importance is 'Conversation in the Mountains'. He
cites it in 'The Meridian' as his counterpart to
Büchner's *Lenz* — and as an encounter with
himself. It is a text which addresses more directly
than Celan's poems the condition of being Jewish,
of being a stranger. A stranger not only in the
social and cultural world: there is a veil between
him and nature, between him and everything. He
always finds himself face to face with the incom-
prehensible, inaccessible, the 'language of the
stone'. And his only recourse is talking. This

cannot be 'literature'. Literature belongs to those who are at home in the world. He can only talk in a simple — deceptively simple — way: circular, repetitive, insisting on the very gap between him and the world, between him and nature. He can only hope that out of his insistence will come a new language which can fill the gap and include the other side. 'Reality must be searched for and won.'

Small wonder that Celan refuses to talk 'technique', that he is contemptuous of the professionals of 'literature' stirring up their 'flurries of metaphor'. Craft is a prerequisite for him, like cleanliness, not worth discussing. He admits exercises, but only 'in the spiritual sense'. Here we are at the core of Celan's relation to writing. It was not a game for him, not experiment, not even 'work'. Writing, as he tells us in 'The Meridian', meant putting his existence on the line, pushing out into regions of the mind where one is exposed to the radically strange, the terrifying other, the uncanny. And at the moment when existence is actually threatened, when his breath fails, when silence literally (if momentarily) means death — at this moment a poem may be born. If so, it pulls us back from the 'already-no-more' into resuming breath and life.

For this moment, this death-in-life when our breath is taken away, yet turns and re-turns, Celan coins the word *Atemwende*. Crucial word which appears here for the first time, before he makes it the title of one of his books. Language is breathing for Celan, is life, is 'direction and destiny'; and the poem, that which takes our breath away, yet gives it back and allows us to live. Just as, on a smaller scale, the constant *Atemwende* we know, the constant alternation of inhaling and exhaling, allows us to practise the encounter with both air and its absence, the condition of our life and the 'other' which will eventually end it.

Celan's prose is a poet's prose. It often progresses by sound association and puns which must suffer in translation. The 'Wände und Einwände' of reality is more vivid, with its image of walls, than my 'objects and objections'. Because 'boat' and 'messenger' do not have the punning connection of 'Boot' and 'Bote', I had to have my boat carried by the tide to make for a similar progression to 'tidings'. Elsewhere I had to introduce an extra sentence to get both the image and the meaning of the German, thus losing the pregnant formulation. But I think I have succeeded in the more important task of staying as true as possible to the varying rhythms. The repetitive and incantatory 'Conversation in the Mountains', for instance, could not be more different from the groping complexity of 'The Meridian', which forever qualifies what is said, while holding on to its anchor: the phrase 'Ladies and gentlemen', the situation of speaking, of addressing a 'you'.

The arrangement of the texts follows Volume Three of Paul Celan's *Gesammelte Werke*, edited by Beda Allemann and Klaus Reichert (Frankfurt:

Suhrkamp, 1983), which divides the works into two chronological sections of 'prose' and 'speeches', leaving the introductory notes to Celan's translations of Blok and Mandelstam for an appendix in Volume Five.

Titles which are not by Celan appear in parentheses, notes added by the editors, in italics.

Rosmarie Waldrop

Prose

Edgar Jené and the Dream about the Dream

I am supposed to tell you some of the words I heard deep down in the sea where there is so much silence and so much happens. I cut my way through the objects and objections of reality and stood before the sea's mirror surface. I had to wait until it burst open and allowed me to enter the huge crystal of the inner world. With the large lower star of disconsolate explorers shining above me, I followed Edgar Jené beneath his paintings.

Though I had known the journey would be strenuous, I worried when I had to enter one of the roads alone, without a guide. One of the roads! There were innumerable, all inviting, all offering me different new eyes to look at the beautiful wilderness on the other, deeper side of existence. No wonder that, in this moment when I still had my own stubborn old eyes, I tried to make comparisons in order to be able to choose. My mouth, however, placed higher than my eyes and bolder for having often spoken in my sleep, had moved ahead and mocked me: 'Well, old identity-monger, what did you see and recognize, you brave doctor of tautology? What could you recognize, tell me, along this unfamiliar road? An also-tree or almost-tree, right? And now you are mustering your Latin for a letter to old Linnaeus? You had better haul up a pair of eyes from the bottom of your soul and put them on your chest: then you'll find out what is happening here.'

Now I am a person who likes simple words. It is true, I had realized long before this journey that there was much evil and injustice in the world I had now left, but I had believed I could shake the foundations if I called things by their proper names. I knew such an enterprise meant returning to absolute *naïveté*. This *naïveté* I considered as a primal vision purified of the slag of centuries of hoary lies about the world. I remember a conversation with a friend about Kleist's *Marionette Theatre*. How could one regain that original grace, which would become the heading of the last and, I suppose, loftiest chapter in the history of mankind? It was, my friend held, by letting reason purify our unconscious inner life that we could recapture the immediacy of the beginning — which would in the end give meaning to our life and make it worth living. In this view, beginning and end were one, and a note of mourning for original sin was struck. The wall which separates today from tomorrow must be torn down so that tomorrow could again be yesterday. But what must we actually do now, in our own time, to reach timelessness, eternity, the marriage of tomorrow-and-yesterday? Reason, he said, must prevail. A bath in the *aqua regia* of intelligence must give their true (primitive) meaning back to words, hence to things, beings, occurrences. A tree must again be a tree, and its branch, on which the rebels of a hundred wars have been hanged, must again flower in spring.

Here my first objection came up. It was simply this: I knew that anything that happened was more than an addition to the given, more than an attribute more or less difficult to remove from the essence, that it changed the essence in its very being and thus cleared the way for ceaseless transformation.

My friend was stubborn. He claimed that even in the stream of human evolution he could distinguish the constants of the soul, know the limits of the unconscious. All we needed was for reason to go down into the deep and haul the water of the dark well up to the surface. This well, like any other, had a bottom one could reach, and if only the surface were ready to receive the water from the deep, the sun of justice shining, the job would be done. But how can we ever succeed, he said, if you and people like you never come out of the deep, never stop communing with the dark springs?

I saw that this reproach was aimed at my professing that, since we know the world and its institutions are a prison for man and his spirit, we must do all we can to tear down its walls. At the

5

same time, I saw which course this knowledge prescribed. I realized that man was not only languishing in the chains of external life, but was also gagged and unable to speak — and by speaking I mean the entire sphere of human expression — because his words (gestures, movements) groaned under an age-old load of false and distorted sincerity. What could be more dishonest than to claim that words had somehow, at bottom, remained the same! I could not help seeing that the ashes of burned-out meanings (and not only of those) had covered what had, since time immemorial, been striving for expression in man's innermost soul.

How could something new and pure issue from this? It may be from the remotest regions of the spirit that words and figures will come, images and gestures, veiled and unveiled as in a dream. When they meet in their heady course, and the spark of the wonderful is born from the marriage of strange and most strange, then I will know I am facing the new radiance. It will give me a dubious look because, even though I have conjured it up, it exists beyond the concepts of my wakeful thinking; its light is not daylight; it is inhabited by figures which I do not *recognize*, but *know* at first sight. Its weight has a different heaviness; its colour speaks to the new eyes which my closed lids have given one another; my hearing has wandered into my fingertips and learns to see; my heart, now that it lives behind my forehead, tastes the laws of a new, unceasing, free motion. I follow my wandering senses into this new world of the spirit and come to know freedom. Here, where I am free, I can see what nasty lies the other side told me.

Thus I listened to my own thoughts during that last break, before facing the dangers of tramping the deep sea, of following Edgar Jené down underneath his paintings.

A Sail Leaves an Eye. One sail only? No, I see two. But the first one, which still bears the colour of the eye, cannot proceed. I know it must come back. Arduous, this return. All liquid has run out of the eye in the form of a steep waterfall. But down here (up there), the water also flows uphill, the sail climbs the steep incline of the white profile which owns nothing but this eye without a pupil and which, just because it owns nothing but this, knows and can do more than we. For this profile of a woman with hair a little bluer than her mouth (which looks up, diagonally, at a mirror we cannot see, tests its expression and judges it appropriate), this profile is a cliff, an icy monument at the access to the inner sea which is a sea of wavy tears. What can the other side of this face look like? Grey like the land we glimpse? But let us go back to our sails. The first one will come home, into the empty, yet strangely seeing socket. Perhaps the tide will carry it in the wrong direction, into the eye which stares out on the grey of the other side . . . Then the boat will bear tidings, but without much promise. And the second boat whose sail bears a fiery eye, a flaming pupil on a field, *sable*, of certainty? We enter it in our sleep: then we see what remains to be dreamed.

How many people know that the number of creatures is endless? That man created them all? May we even begin to count them? True, some know that you can give a flower to a person. But how many know that you can also give a person to a pink? And which do they consider more important? More than one will remain incredulous when you mention the son of Aurora Borealis.

Incredulous even today, when Berenice's hair has been hanging among the stars for such a long time. However, Aurora Borealis does have a son, and Edgar Jené has been the first to see him. Where man is frozen and chained in the snowy woods of his despair, he passes by. Huge. Trees do not stop him. He steps across or takes them under his wide cloak, makes them his companions on the way to the city gates where people wait for the great brother. He is the one expected. We know it by his eyes: they have seen what all have seen, and then some.

What Edgar Jené gives shape to — is its home only here? Have we not all wanted to know better the nightmare of the old reality? Have we not wanted to hear screams, our own screams louder than ever, more piercing? Look, this mirror below us makes everything show its true colour: *The Sea of Blood Covers the Land.* Devastated and grey, the hills of life. With naked feet, the spectre of war goes through the land. Now it has claws like a bird of prey, now human toes. Many are its shapes. Which one is it wearing now? A tent of blood floating in the air. Wherever it comes down, we must live between walls and shreds of blood. Where blood yawns, we get a chance to look out and see more of the same shapes of steaming blood. And we are fed: one of the claws has drilled a well of blood. There we can also mirror ourselves, lost as we are. Blood in a mirror of blood, what greater beauty, they say . . .

———

Many oaths have we sworn in our waking lives, in the hot shadow of impatient flags, backlighted by an alien death, at the high altar of our sanctified reason. We kept our pledges at the cost of our secret life. But when we came back to where we had made them — what did we find? The colour of the flag was the same, the shadow it threw even larger than before. Again, people raised their hands. But to whom did they pledge allegiance? To the Other, whom we had sworn to hate. And death, the alien? It was so busy it had no need of our oaths at all . . . On the altar, finally, a cock, crowing.

Now let us try to make pledges in our sleep. We are forming a tower, our face breaking through at the top, our clenched stone face. Taller than ourselves, we tower above the highest towers and can look down on ourselves, on our thousand-fold climb upwards. What a chance: to gather in hordes up there to swear our oaths, a thousand times ourselves, a great, overwhelming force. We have not quite reached the top, where our face has already become a clenched fist, a fist of eyes swearing. But we can see our way. Steep, the ascent. But if it is to tomorrow's truth that we want to pledge allegiance we must take this route. And once up there! What a site for an oath! What a climb into the deep! What resonance for the pledge we do not know yet!

I have tried to report some of what I saw in the deep sea of a soul.

Edgar Jené's paintings know more.

Backlight

The heart hid still in the dark, hard as the Philosopher's Stone.

———

Spring: trees flying up to their birds.

———

The pitcher which went to the well once too often still gets by, but the well runs dry.

———

Our talk of justice is empty until the largest battleship has foundered on the forehead of a drowned man.

———

Four seasons, but no fifth to give our choice perspective.

———

So strong was his love for her it would have pushed open the lid of his coffin — had the flower she placed there not been so heavy.

———

Love despaired of them: so long was their embrace.

———

The day of judgement had come. In order to find the greatest crime the cross was nailed to Christ.

———

Bury the flower and put a man on its grave.

———

The hour jumped out of the clock, stood facing it, and ordered it to work properly.

———

When the general laid the rebel's bloody head at the feet of his sovereign, the latter flew into a rage.

'How dare you fill the throne chamber with the stink of blood,' he cried, and the general trembled.

The slain man opened his mouth and told the story of the lilac tree.

'Too late,' guessed the chamberlains.

A later chronicler confirmed their opinion.

———

When the hanged man was taken down from the gallows his eyes were still unbroken. The executioner hastened to close them, but the bystanders had noticed and lowered their own eyes in shame.

The gallows, however, for this one minute, considered itself a tree, and as nobody had looked up we cannot be sure that it was not.

———

He put his virtues and vices, his innocence and guilt, his good and bad qualities on the scales because he wanted certainty before judging himself. But piled this way, the scales balanced.

As he wanted to know at any price, he shut his eyes and walked in circles around the scales, now clockwise, now counterclockwise, until he no longer knew which of the pans held which load. Then he blindly put on one of them his decision to judge himself.

Sure enough, when he opened his eyes again, one arm had gone down. But there was no way of knowing which: the scale of guilt or the scale of innocence.

This made him furious. He refused to see the advantage of the situation and sentenced himself — without, however, being able to shake off the feeling that he might be doing himself an injustice.

Do not be deceived: this last lamp does not give more light — the dark has only become more absorbed in itself.

'All things are aflowing': this thought included — and does that not bring everything to a halt?

She turned her back on the mirror, hating the mirror's vanity.

He taught the Law of Gravity, furnished proof after proof, but people turned deaf ears. Then he took off into the air and, floating there, repeated the lesson. Now people believed. But nobody was surprised when he did not come down again.

[Reply to a Questionnaire from the Flinker Bookstore, Paris, 1958]

The questionnaire asked philosophers and writers for information about their work in progress.

You have been kind enough to ask about my present work and projects. But your question comes to an author whose publications to date are three books of poems. It is only as a poet that I can try to answer and keep within your framework.

German poetry is going in a very different direction from French poetry. No matter how alive its traditions, with most sinister events in its memory, most questionable developments around it, it can no longer speak the language which many willing ears seem to expect. Its language has become more sober, more factual. It distrusts 'beauty'. It tries to be truthful. If I may search for a visual analogy while keeping in mind the poly-chrome of apparent actuality: it is a 'greyer' language, a language which wants to locate even its 'musicality' in such a way that it has nothing in common with the 'euphony' which more or less blithely continued to sound alongside the greatest horrors. This language, notwithstanding its inalienable complexity of expression, is concerned with precision. It does not transfigure or render 'poetical'; it names, it posits, it tries to measure the area of the given and the possible. True, this is never the working of language itself, language as such, but always of an 'I' who speaks from the particular angle of reflection which is his existence and who is concerned with outlines and orientation. Reality is not simply there, it must be searched and won.

But am I still anywhere near your question? Those poets! One ends up wishing that, some day, they might manage to get a solid novel on to paper.

Conversation in the Mountains

One evening, when the sun had set and not only
the sun, the Jew — Jew and son of a Jew — went
off, left his house and went off, and with him his
name, his unpronounceable name, went and came,
came trotting along, made himself heard, came
with a stick, came over stones, do you hear me,
you do, it's me, me, me and whom you hear,
whom you think you hear, me and the other — so
he went off, you could hear it, went off one
evening when various things had set, went under
clouds, went in the shadow, his own and not his
own — because the Jew, you know, what does he
have that is really his own, that is not borrowed,
taken and not returned — so he went off and
walked along this road, this beautiful, incom-
parable road, walked like Lenz through the mountains, he who had been allowed to live down in the
plain where he belongs, he, the Jew, walked and
walked.

Walked, yes, along this road, this beautiful road. And who do you think came to meet him? His cousin came to meet him, his first cousin, a quarter of a Jew's life older, tall he came, came, he too, in the shadow, borrowed of course — because, I ask and ask you, how could he come with his own when God had made him a Jew — came, tall, came to meet the other, Gross approached Klein, and Klein, the Jew, silenced his stick before the stick of the Jew Gross.

The stones, too, were silent. And it was quiet in the mountains where they walked, one and the other.

So it was quiet, quiet up there in the mountains. But it was not quiet for long, because when a Jew comes along and meets another, silence cannot last, even in the mountains. Because the Jew and nature are strangers to each other, have always been and still are, even today, even here.

So there they are, the cousins. On the left, the turk's-cap lily blooms, blooms wild, blooms like nowhere else. And on the right, corn-salad, and *dianthus superbus*, the maiden-pink, not far off. But they, those cousins, have no eyes, alas. Or, more exactly: they have, even they have eyes, but with a veil hanging in front of them, no, not in front, behind them, a moveable veil. No sooner does an image enter than it gets caught in the web, and a thread starts spinning, spinning itself around the image, a veil-thread; spins itself around the image and begets a child, half image, half veil.

18

Poor lily, poor corn-salad. There they stand, the cousins, on a road in the mountains, the stick silent, the stones silent, and the silence no silence at all. No word has come to an end and no phrase, it is nothing but a pause, an empty space between the words, a blank — you see all the syllables stand around, waiting. They are tongue and mouth as before, these two, and in their eyes there hangs a veil, and you, poor flowers, are not even there, are not blooming, you do not exist, and July is not July.

The windbags! Even now, when their tongues stumble dumbly against their teeth and their lips won't round themselves, they have something to say to each other. All right then, let them talk . . .

"You've come a long way, have come all the way here . . .'

'I have. I've come, like you.'

'I know.'

'You know. You know and see: The earth folded up here, folded once and twice and three times, and opened up in the middle, and in the middle there is water, and the water is green, and the green is white, and the white comes from even farther up, from the glaciers, and one could say, but one shouldn't, that this is the language that counts here, the green with the white in it, a language not for you and not for me — because, I ask you, for whom is it meant, the earth, not for you, I say, is it meant, and not for me — a language, well, without I and without You, nothing but He, nothing but It, you understand, and She, nothing but that.'

'I understand, I do. After all, I've come a long way, I've come like you.'

'I know.'

'You know and you want to ask: And even so you've come all the way, come here even so — why, and what for?'

'Why, and what for . . . Because I had to talk, maybe, to myself or to you, talk with my mouth and tongue, not just with my stick. Because to whom does it talk, my stick? It talks to the stones, and the stones — to whom do they talk?'

'To whom should they talk, cousin? They do not talk, they speak, and who speaks does not talk to anyone, cousin, he speaks because nobody hears him, nobody and Nobody, and then he says, himself, not his mouth or his tongue, he, and only he, says: Do you hear me?'

'Do you hear me, he says — I know, cousin, I know . . . Do you hear me, he says, I'm here. I am here, I've come. I've come with my stick, me and no other, me and not him, me with my hour, my undeserved hour, me who have been hit, who have not been hit, me with my memory, with my lack of memory, me, me, me . . .'

'He says, he says . . . Do you hear me, he says . . . And Do-you-hear-me, of course, Do-you-hear-me does not say anything, does not answer, because Do-you-hear-me is one with the glaciers, is three in one, and not for men . . . The green-and-white there, with the turk's-cap lily, with the corn-salad . . . But I, cousin, I who stand here on this road, here where I do not belong, today, now that it has set, the sun and its light, I, here, with the shadow, my own and not my own, I — I who can tell you:

'I lay on the stones, back then, you know, on the stone tiles; and next to me the others who were like me, the others who were different and yet like me, my cousins. They lay there sleeping, sleeping and not sleeping, dreaming and not dreaming, and they did not love me, and I did not love them because I was one, and who wants to love One when there are many, even more than those lying near me, and who wants to be able to love all, and I don't hide it from you, I did not love them who could not love me, I loved the candle which burned in the left corner, I loved it because it burned down, not because *it* burned down, because *it* was *his* candle, the candle he had lit, our mothers' father, because on that evening there had begun a day, a particular day: the seventh, the seventh to be followed by the first, the seventh and not the last, cousin, I did not love *it*, I loved its burning down and, you know, I haven't loved anything since.

'No. Nothing. Or maybe whatever burned down like that candle on that day, the seventh, not the last; not on the last day, no, because here I am, here on this road which they say is beautiful, here I am, by the turk's-cap lily and the corn-salad, and a hundred yards over, over there where I could go, the larch gives way to the stone-pine, I see it, I see it and don't see it, and my stick which talked to the stones, my stick is silent now, and the stones you say can speak, and in my eyes there is that moveable veil, there are veils, moveable veils, you lift one, and there hangs another, and the star there — yes, it is up there now, above the mountains — if it wants to enter it will have to wed and soon it won't be itself, but half veil and half star, and I know, I know, cousin, I know I've met you here, and we talked, a lot, and those folds there, you know they are not for men, and not for us who went off and met here, under the star, we the Jews who came like Lenz through the mountains, you Gross and me Klein, you, the windbag, and me, the windbag, with our sticks, with our unpronounceable names, with our shadows, our own and not our own, you here and me here —

'me here, me, who can tell you all this, could have and don't and didn't tell you; me with a turk's-cap lily on my left, me with corn-salad, me with my burned candle, me with the day, me with the days, me here and there, me, maybe accompanied — now — by the love of those I didn't love, me on the way to myself, up here.'

August 1959

[Reply to a Questionnaire from the Flinker Bookstore, Paris, 1961]

The subject of the study was 'The Problem of the Bilingual'.

You inquire into language, into thinking, into poetry. You put your question succinctly. Allow me to be as succinct in my answer.

I do not believe there is such a thing as bilingual poetry. Double-talk, yes, this you may find among our various contemporary arts and acrobatics of the word, especially those which manage to establish themselves in blissful harmony with each fashion of consumer culture, being as polyglot as they are polychrome.

Poetry is by necessity a unique instance of language. Hence never — forgive the truism, but poetry, like truth, goes all too often to the dogs — hence never what is double.

[Letter to Hans Bender]

Dear Hans Bender,

thank you for your letter of May 15 and your friendly invitation to contribute to your anthology, *My Poem Is my Knife*.

I remember telling you that once the poem is really *there*, the poet is dismissed, is no longer privy. Today, I suppose I would formulate it differently, with more nuances, but in principle I still hold this — old — view. True, there is the aspect which people currently, and so blithely, like to call *craft*. But — if you will allow me to condense much thinking and experience — craft, like cleanliness in general, is the condition of all poetry. *This* craft most certainly does not bring monetary rewards, does not have the 'golden bottom' of the proverb. Who knows if it has any bottom at all. It has its depths and abysses — and some people (alas, I am not among them) even have a name for that.

Craft means handiwork, a matter of hands. And these hands must belong to *one* person, i.e. a unique, mortal soul searching for its way with its voice and its dumbness. Only truthful hands write true poems. I cannot see any basic difference between a handshake and a poem.

Don't come with *poiein* and the like. I suspect that this word, with all its nearness and distance, meant something quite different from its current context.

True, there are exercises — in the *spiritual* sense, dear Hans Bender. And then there are, at every lyrical street corner, experiments that muck around with the so-called word-material. Poems are also gifts — gifts to the attentive. Gifts bearing destinies.

'How are poems made?'

Some years ago, I had the occasion to witness and, later, to watch from a certain distance how 'making' turns by and by into 'making it' and thence into machinations. Yes, there is *this*, too. Perhaps you know about it. It does not happen by accident.

We live under dark skies and — there are few human beings. Hence, I assume, so few poems. The hopes I have left are small. I try to hold on to what remains.

With all good wishes for you and your work,

your Paul Celan

Paris, 18 May 1960

[Reply to a Poll by *Der Spiegel*]

Under the heading, 'Is a Revolution Unavoidable?'
the magazine had asked for positions on the
alternative Hans Magnus Enzensberger had
formulated in the Times Literary Supplement:
'. . . in fact, we are not confronting communism,
but revolution. The political system of the German
Federal Republic is irreparable. We can either
accept it or replace it with a new system. Tertium
non dabitur.'

I still hope, and not only in regard to the Federal
Republic and Germany, for change, for transformation. Substitute systems will not bring it about,
and revolution — a social and at the same time
anti-authoritarian one — can only be conceived
with change as its basis. It begins, in Germany,
here, today, with the individual. May we be spared
a fourth possibility.

La poésie ne s'impose plus, elle s'expose.
26 March 1969

Speeches

Speech on the Occasion of Receiving the Literature Prize of the Free Hanseatic City of Bremen

The words 'denken' and 'danken', to think and to thank, have the same root in our language. If we follow it to 'gedenken', 'eingedenk sein', 'Andenken' and 'Andacht' we enter the semantic fields of memory and devotion. Allow me to thank you from there.

The region from which I come to you — with what detours! but then, is there such a thing as a detour? — will be unfamiliar to most of you. It is the home of many of the Hassidic stories which Martin Buber has retold in German. It was — if I may flesh out this topographical sketch with a few details which are coming back to me from a great distance — it was a landscape where both people and books lived. There, in this former province of the Habsburg monarchy, now dropped from history, I first encountered the name of Rudolf Alexander Schröder while reading Rudolf Borchardt's 'Ode with Pomegranate'. There, the word

Bremen took shape for me: in the publications of the 'Bremer Presse'.

But though Bremen was brought closer through books, through the names of writers and publishers of books, it still had the sound of the unreachable.

Within reach, though far enough, what I could aim to reach, was Vienna. You know what happened, in the years to come, even to this nearness.

Only one thing remained reachable, close and secure amid all losses: language. Yes, language. In spite of everything, it remained secure against loss. But it had to go through its own lack of answers, through terrifying silence, through the thousand darknesses of murderous speech. It went through. It gave me no words for what was happening, but went through it. Went through and could resurface, 'enriched' by it all.

In this language I tried, during those years and the years after, to write poems: in order to speak, to orient myself, to find out where I was, where I was going, to chart my reality.

It meant movement, you see, something happening, being *en route*, an attempt to find a direction. Whenever I ask about the sense of it, I remind myself that this implies the question as to which sense is clockwise.

For the poem does not stand outside time. True, it claims the infinite and tries to reach across time — but across, not above.

A poem, being an instance of language, hence

34

essentially dialogue, may be a letter in a bottle thrown out to sea with the — surely not always strong — hope that it may somehow wash up somewhere, perhaps on a shoreline of the heart. In this way, too, poems are *en route*: they are headed toward.

Toward what? Toward something open, inhabitable, an approachable you, perhaps, an approachable reality.

Such realities are, I think, at stake in a poem.

I also believe that this kind of thinking accompanies not only my own efforts, but those of other, younger poets. Efforts of those who, with manmade stars flying overhead, unsheltered even by the traditional tent of the sky, exposed in an unsuspected, terrifying way, carry their existence into language, racked by reality and in search of it.

The Meridian

*Speech on the occasion of receiving the Georg
Büchner Prize, Darmstadt, 22 October 1960*

Ladies and Gentlemen,

Art, you will remember, is a puppet-like, iambic,
five-footed thing without — and this last charac-
teristic has its mythological validation in Pyg-
malion and his statue — without offspring.

In this form, it is the subject of a conversation in
Danton's Death which takes place in a room, not
yet in the Conciergerie, a conversation which, we
feel, could go on forever if there were no snags.

There are snags.

Art comes up again. It comes up in another work
of Georg Büchner's, in *Woyzeck*, among other,
nameless people in a yet more 'ashen light before
the storm' — if I may use the phrase Moritz
Heimann intended for *Danton's Death*. Here, in
very different times, art comes presented by a
carnival barker and has no longer, as in that
conversation, anything to do with 'glowing',

37

'roaring', 'radiant' creation, but is put next to the 'creature as God made it' and the 'nothing' this creature is 'wearing'. This time, art comes in the shape of a monkey. But it is art all right. We recognize it by its 'coat and trousers'.

It — art — comes to us in yet a third play of Büchner's, in *Leonce and Lena*. Time and lighting are unrecognizable: we are 'fleeing towards paradise'; and 'all clocks and calendars' are soon to be 'broken' or, rather, 'forbidden'. But just before that moment, 'two persons of the two sexes' are introduced: 'two world-famous automatons have arrived'. And a man who claims to be 'the third and perhaps strangest of the two' invites us, 'with a rattling voice', to admire what we see: 'Nothing but art and mechanics, nothing but cardboard and springs.'

Art appears here in larger company than before, but obviously of its own sort. It is the same art: art as we already know it. Valerio is only another name for the barker.

Art, ladies and gentlemen, with all its attributes and future additions, is also a problem and, as we can see, one that is variable, tough, longlived, let us say, eternal.

A problem which allows a mortal, Camille, and a man whom we can only understand through his death, Danton, to join word to word to word. It is easy to talk about art.

But when there is talk of art, there is often somebody who does not really listen.

More precisely: somebody who hears, listens, looks . . . and then does not know what it was about. But who hears the speaker, 'sees him speaking', who perceives language as a physical shape and also — who could doubt it within Büchner's work — breath, that is, direction and destiny.

I am talking — you have long guessed it as she comes to you year after year, not by accident quoted so frequently — I am talking of Lucile.

The snags which halt the conversation in *Danton's Death* are brutal. They take us to the *Place de la Révolution*: 'the carts drive up and stop.'

They are all there, Danton, Camille, and the rest. They do not lack words, even here, artful, resonant words, and they get them out. Words — in places Büchner need only quote — about going to their death together; Fabre would even like to die 'twice'; everybody rises to the occasion. Only a few voices, 'some' — unnamed — 'voices', find they 'have heard it before, it is boring'.

And here where it all comes to an end, in those long last moments when Camille — no, not *the* Camille, a fellow prisoner — when this other Camille dies a theatrical, I am tempted to say iambic death which we only two scenes later come to feel as his own, through another person's words, not his, yet kin — here where it all comes to its end, where all around Camille pathos and sententiousness confirm the triumph of 'puppet' and 'string', here Lucile who is blind against art, Lucile for whom language is tangible and like a person, Lucile is suddenly there with her 'Long live the king!'

After all those words on the platform (the guillotine, mind you) — what a word!

It is a word against the grain, the word which cuts the 'string', which does not bow to the 'bystanders and old warhorses of history'. It is an act of freedom. It is a step.

True, it sounds — and in the context of what I now, today, dare say about it, this is perhaps no accident — it sounds at first like allegiance to the 'ancien régime'.

But it is not. Allow me, who grew up on the writings of Peter Kropotkin and Gustav Landauer, to insist: this is not homage to any monarchy, to any yesterday worth preserving.

It is homage to the majesty of the absurd which bespeaks the presence of human beings.

This, ladies and gentlemen, has no definitive name, but I believe that this is . . . poetry.

'Oh, art!' You see I am stuck on this word of Camille's.

I know we can read it in different ways, we can give it a variety of accents: the acute of the present, the grave accent of history (literary history included), the circumflex (marking length) of eternity.

I give it — I have no other choice — I give it an
acute accent.

Art — 'oh, art!' — beside being changeable, has the
gift of ubiquity. We find it again in *Lenz*, but, let
me stress this, as in *Danton's Death*, only as an
episode.

'Over dinner, Lenz recovered his spirits: they
talked literature, he was in his element . . .'
'. . . The feeling that there is life in a work was
more important than those other two, was the
only criterion in matters of art . . .'

I picked only two sentences. My bad conscience
about the grave accent bids me draw your attention to their importance in literary history. We
must read this passage together with the conversation in *Danton's Death*. Here, Büchner's aes-
thetics finds expression. It leads us from the *Lenz*
fragment to Reinhold Lenz, author of *Notes on the
Theatre*, and, back beyond the historical Lenz, to
Mercier's seminal 'Elargissez l'art.' This passage
opens vistas: it anticipates Naturalism and Gerhart
Hauptmann. Here we must look for the social and
political roots of Büchner's work, and here we will
find them.

Ladies and gentlemen, it has, if only for a moment,
calmed my conscience that I did not fail to mention all this. But it also shows, and thereby dis-
turbs my conscience again, that I cannot get away

from something which seems connected with art.

I am looking for it here, in *Lenz* — now you are forewarned.

Lenz, that is, Büchner, has ('oh, art') only contemptuous words for 'idealism' and its 'wooden puppets'. He contrasts it with what is natural for the creature and follows up with his unforgettable lines about the 'life of the least of beings', the 'tremors and hints', the 'subtle, hardly noticeable play of expressions on his face'. And he illustrates this view of art with a scene he has witnessed:

> As I was walking in the valley yesterday, I saw two girls sitting on a rock. One was putting up her hair, and the other helped. The golden hair hanging down, and a pale, serious face, so very young, and the black dress, and the other girl so careful and attentive. Even the finest, most intimate paintings of the old German masters can hardly give you an idea of the scene. Sometimes one would like to be a Medusa's head to turn such a group to stone and gather the people around it.

Please note, ladies and gentlemen: 'One would like to be a Medusa's head' to . . . seize the natural as the natural by means of art!

One would like to, by the way, not: *I* would.

This means going beyond what is human, stepping into a realm which is turned toward the human, but uncanny — the realm where the monkey, the automatons and with them . . . oh, art, too, seem to be at home.

This is not the historical Lenz speaking, but Büchner's. Here we hear Büchner's own voice: here, as in his other works, art has its uncanny side.

Ladies and gentlemen, I have placed my acute accent. I cannot hide from you any more than from myself that, if I took my question about art and poetry, a question among others, if I took it of my own — though perhaps not free — will to Büchner, it was in order to find his way of asking it.

But you see: we cannot ignore the 'rattling' voice Valerio gets whenever art is mentioned.

This uncanny, Büchner's voice leads me to suppose, takes us far, very far back. And it must be in the air — the air we have to breathe — that I so stubbornly insist on it today.

Now I must ask, does Büchner, the poet of the creature, not call art into question, and from this direction? A challenge perhaps muted, perhaps only half conscious, but for all that — perhaps because of that — no less essentially radical? A challenge to which all poetry must return if it wants to question further? In other words (and leaving out some of the steps): may we, like many of our contemporaries, take art for granted, for absolutely given? Should we, to put it concretely, should we think Mallarmé, for instance, through to the end?

I have jumped ahead, reached beyond my topic, though not far enough, I know. Let me return to Büchner's *Lenz*, to the (episodic) conversation 'over dinner' during which Lenz 'recovered his spirits'. Lenz talked for a long time, 'now smiling, now serious'. And when the conversation is over, Büchner says of him, of the man who thinks about questions of art, but also of Lenz, the artist: 'He had forgotten all about himself.'

I think of Lucile when I read this. I read: *He*, he himself.

The man whose eyes and mind are occupied with art — I am still with *Lenz* — forgets about himself. Art makes for distance from the I. Art requires that we travel a certain space in a certain direction, on a certain road.

And poetry? Poetry which, of course, must go the way of art? Here this would actually mean the road to Medusa's head and the automaton!

I am not looking for a way out, I am only pushing the question farther in the same direction which is, I think, also the direction of the *Lenz* fragment..

Perhaps — I am only speculating — perhaps poetry, like art, moves with the oblivious self into the uncanny and strange to free itself. Though where? in which place? how? as what? This would mean art is the distance poetry must cover, no less and no more.

I know there are other, shorter routes. But poetry, too, can be ahead. *La poésie, elle aussi, brûle nos étapes.*

I will now leave the man who has forgotten about himself, who thinks about art, the artist. I believe that I have met poetry in the figure of Lucile, and Lucile perceives language as shape, direction, breath. I am looking for the same thing here, in Büchner's work. I am looking for Lenz himself, as a person, I am looking for his shape: for the sake of the place of poetry, for the sake of liberation, for the sake of the step.

Büchner's *Lenz* has remained a fragment, ladies and gentlemen. Shall we look at the historical Lenz in order to find out what direction this life had?

'His existence was a necessary burden for him. Thus he lived on . . .' Here the tale breaks off.

But poetry, like Lucile, tries to see the figure in his direction. Poetry rushes ahead. We know how he lives *on, on toward* what.

'Death,' we read in a work on Jakob Michael Reinhold Lenz published in Leipzig, in 1909, from the pen of a Moscow professor, M. N. Rosanow, 'death was not slow to deliver him. In the night from the 23rd to the 24th of May, 1792, Lenz was found dead in a street in Moscow. A nobleman paid for his funeral. His grave has remained unknown.'

45

Thus *he* had lived *on*.

He: the real Lenz, Büchner's figure, the person whom we encountered on the first page of the story, the Lenz who 'on the 20th of January was walking through the mountains', he — not the artist thinking about art — he as an 'I'.

Can we perhaps now locate the strangeness, the place where the person was able to set himself free as an — estranged — I? Can we locate this place, this step?

'. . . only, it sometimes bothered him that he could not walk on his head.' This is Lenz. This is, I believe, his step, his 'Long live the king'.

'. . . only, it sometimes bothered him that he could not walk on his head.'

A man who walks on his head, ladies and gentlemen, a man who walks on his head sees the sky below, as an abyss.

Ladies and gentlemen, it is very common today to complain of the 'obscurity' of poetry. Allow me to quote, a bit abruptly — but do we not have a sudden opening here? — a phrase of Pascal's which I read in Leo Shestov: 'Ne nous reprochez pas le manque de clarté puisque nous en faisons profession.' This obscurity, if it is not congenital, has been bestowed on poetry by strangeness and distance (perhaps of its own making) and for the sake of an encounter.

But there may be, in one and the same direction, two kinds of strangeness next to each other.

Lenz — that is, Büchner — has gone a step farther than Lucile. His 'Long live the king' is no longer a word. It is a terrifying silence. It takes his — and our — breath and words away.

Poetry is perhaps this: an *Atemwende*, a turning of our breath. Who knows, perhaps poetry goes its way — the way of art — for the sake of just such a turn? And since the strange, the abyss *and* Medusa's head, the abyss *and* the automaton, all seem to lie in the same direction — it is perhaps this turn, this *Atemwende*, which can sort out the strange from the strange? It is perhaps here, in this one brief moment, that Medusa's head shrivels and the automatons run down? Perhaps, along with the I, estranged and freed *here, in this manner*, some other thing is also set free?

Perhaps after this, the poem can be itself . . . can in this now art-less, art-free manner go other ways, including the ways of art, time and again?

Perhaps.

Perhaps we can say that every poem is marked by its own '20th of January'? Perhaps the newness of poems written today is that they try most plainly to be mindful of this kind of date?

But do we not all write from and toward some such date? What else could we claim as our origin?

But the poem speaks. It is mindful of its dates, but it speaks. True, it speaks only on its own, its very own behalf.

But I think — and this will hardly surprise you — that the poem has always hoped, for this very reason, to speak also on behalf of the *strange* — no, I can no longer use this word here — *on behalf of the other*, who knows, perhaps of an *altogether other*.

This 'who knows' which I have reached is all I can add here, today, to the old hopes.

Perhaps, I am led to speculate, perhaps an encounter is conceivable between this 'altogether other' — I am using a familiar auxiliary — and a not so very distant, a quite close 'other' — conceivable, perhaps, again and again.

The poem takes such thoughts for its home and hope — a word for living creatures.

Nobody can tell how long the pause for breath — hope and thought — will last. 'Speed', which has always been 'outside', has gained yet more speed. The poem knows this, but heads straight for the 'otherness' which it considers it can reach and be free, which is perhaps vacant and at the same time turned like Lucile, let us say, turned toward it, toward the poem.

It is true, the poem, the poem today, shows — and this has only indirectly to do with the difficulties of vocabulary, the faster flow of syntax or a more awakened sense of ellipsis, none of which we should underrate — the poem clearly shows a strong tendency towards silence.

The poem holds its ground, if you will permit me yet another extreme formulation, the poem holds its ground on its own margin. In order to endure, it constantly calls and pulls itself back from an 'already-no-more' into a 'still-here'.

This 'still-here' can only mean speaking. Not language as such, but responding and — not just verbally — 'corresponding' to something.

In other words: language actualized, set free under the sign of a radical individuation which, however, remains as aware of the limits drawn by language as of the possibilities it opens.

This 'still-here' of the poem can only be found in the work of poets who do not forget that they speak from an angle of reflection which is their own existence, their own physical nature.

This shows the poem yet more clearly as one person's language becomes shape and, essentially, a presence in the present.

The poem is lonely. It is lonely and *en route*. Its author stays with it.

Does this very fact not place the poem already here, at its inception, in the encounter, *in the mystery of encounter*?

The poem intends another, needs this other, needs an opposite. It goes toward it, bespeaks it.

For the poem, everything and everybody is a figure of this other toward which it is heading.

Paul Celan

The attention which the poem pays to all that it encounters, its more acute sense of detail, outline, structure, colour, but also of the 'tremors and hints' — all this is not, I think, achieved by an eye competing (or concurring) with ever more precise instruments, but, rather, by a kind of concentration mindful of all our dates.

'Attention', if you allow me a quote from Malebranche via Walter Benjamin's essay on Kafka, 'attention is the natural prayer of the soul'.

The poem becomes — under what conditions — the poem of a person who still perceives, still turns towards phenomena, addressing and questioning them. The poem becomes conversation — often desperate conversation.

Only the space of this conversation can establish what is addressed, can gather it into a 'you' around the naming and speaking I. But this 'you', come about by dint of being named and addressed, brings its otherness into the present. Even in the here and now of the poem — and the poem has only this one, unique, momentary present — even in this immediacy and nearness, the otherness gives voice to what is most its own: its time.

Whenever we speak with things in this way we also dwell on the question of their where-from and where-to, an 'open' question 'without resolution', a question which points towards open, empty, free spaces — we have ventured far out.

The poem also searches for this place.

The poem?

The poem with its images and tropes?

Ladies and gentlemen, what am I actually talking about when I speak from *this* position, in *this* direction, with *these* words about the poem, no, about *the* poem?

I am talking about a poem which does not exist!

The absolute poem — no, it certainly does not, cannot exist.

But in every real poem, even the least ambitious, there is this ineluctable question, this exorbitant claim.

Then what are images?

What has been, what can be perceived, again and again, and only here, only now. Hence the poem is the place where all tropes and metaphors want to be led *ad absurdum*.

And topological research?

Certainly. But in the light of what is still to be searched for: in a u-topian light.

And the human being? The physical creature?

In this light.

What questions! What claims!

It is time to retrace our steps.

Ladies and gentlemen, I have come to the end — I have come back to the beginning.

Elargissez l'art! This problem confronts us with its old and new uncanniness. I took it to Büchner, and think I found it in his work.

I even had an answer ready, I wanted to counter, to contradict, with a word against the grain, like Lucile's.

Enlarge art?

No. On the contrary, take art with you into your innermost narrowness. And set yourself free.

I have taken this route, even today, with you. It has been a circle.

Art (this includes Medusa's head, the mechanism, the automaton), art, the uncanny strangeness which is so hard to differentiate and perhaps is only *one* after all — art lives on.

Twice, with Lucile's 'Long live the king' and when the sky opened as an abyss under Lenz, there seemed to occur an *Atemwende*, a turning of breath. Perhaps also while I was trying to head for that inhabitable distance which, finally, was visible only in the figure of Lucile. And once, by dint of attention to things and beings, we came close to a free, open space and, finally, close to utopia.

Poetry, ladies and gentlemen: what an eternalization of nothing but mortality, and in vain.

Ladies and gentlemen, allow me, since I have come back to the beginning, to ask once more, briefly and from a different direction, the same question.

Ladies and gentlemen, several years ago I wrote a little quatrain:

Voices from the path through nettles:
Come to us on your hands.
Alone with your lamp,
Only your hand to read.

And a year ago, I commemorated a missed encounter in the Engadine valley by putting a little story on paper where I had a man 'like Lenz' walk through the mountains.

Both times, I had written from a '20th of January', from my '20th of January'.

I had . . . encountered myself.

Is it on such paths that poems take us when we think of them? And are these paths only detours, detours from you to you? But they are, among how many others, the paths on which language becomes voice. They are encounters, paths from a voice to a listening You, natural paths, outlines for existence perhaps, for projecting ourselves into the search for ourselves . . . A kind of homecoming.

Ladies and gentlemen, I am coming to the end, I am coming, along with my acute accent, to the end of . . . *Leonce and Lena.*

And here, with the last two words of this work, I must be careful.

I must be careful not to misread, as Karl Emil Franzos did (*my rediscovered fellow countryman Karl Emil Franzos*) editor of that 'First Critical and Complete Edition of Georg Büchner's Works

53

and Posthumous Writings' which was published eighty-one years ago by Sauerländer in Frankfurt am Main — I must be careful not to misread *das Commode*, 'the comfort' we now need, as 'the coming thing'.

And yet: is *Leonce and Lena* not full of words which seem to smile through invisible quotation marks, which we should perhaps not call *Gänse-füsschen*, or goose feet, but rather rabbit's ears, that is, something that listens, not without fear, for something beyond itself, beyond words?

From this point of 'comfort', but also in the light of utopia, let me now undertake a bit of topo-logical research. I shall search for the region from which hail Reinhold Lenz and Karl Emil Franzos whom I have met on my way here and in Büchner's work. I am also, since I am again at my point of departure, searching for my own place of origin.

I am looking for all this with my imprecise, because nervous, finger on a map — a child's map, I must admit.

None of these places can be found. They do not exist. But I know where they ought to exist, especially now, and . . . I find something else.

Ladies and gentlemen, I find something which consoles me a bit for having walked this impos-sible road in your presence, this road of the impossible.

I find the connective which, like the poem, leads to encounters.

I find something as immaterial as language, yet earthly, terrestrial, in the shape of a circle which, via both poles, rejoins itself and on the way serenely crosses even the tropics: I find . . . a *meridian*.

With you and Georg Büchner and the State of Hesse, I believe I have just touched it again.

[Address to the Hebrew Writers' Association]

I came to you, to Israel, because I needed you.

I have rarely felt as strongly as now, after all I have seen and heard, that I have done the right thing — I hope not for myself alone.

I believe I have an idea of what Jewish loneliness means, and I understand, among other things, your grateful pride in every bit of green you planted and which now refreshes all that pass by. As I also understand the joy over every newly won, felt and fulfilled word which rushes to sustain the person who turns to it. I understand what all this means in our time of growing masses and alienation. Here, in your inner and outer landscape, I find much of the compulsion toward truth, much of the self-evidence, much of the world-open uniqueness of great poetry. And I believe I have encountered the calm and confident resolution to hold on to what is human.

I am grateful to you, grateful for all this.

Tel-Aviv, 14 October 1969

Appendices

Introductory Notes to the Translations of Blok and Mandelstam

Alexander Blok, one of Russia's greatest poets, was born on 16 November 1880, in St Petersburg. He died on 7 August 1921, in his home town, famous and lonely.

The Twelve, which is, with *The Scythians*, the poet's last work, was written shortly after the October Revolution, in the middle of the civil war, between 8 and 28 January 1918. Written 'in harmony with the elements' (thus a note in his journal), the poem grew from its middle: the eighth section (from 'O grief' to 'desolation') came first. We may consider it the heart of the poem.

Myth? Document? Hymn to, or satire of, the Revolution? Both camps have been able to claim it. Blok himself noted in his journal:

Let's see what time will make of it. Maybe politics is such a dirty thing that even a single drop will muddy and ruin all the rest. Maybe it cannot destroy the sense of the poem even so. And, who knows, perhaps it will prove to be the ferment which will cause *The Twelve* to be re-read in another time . . .

1958

Osip Mandelstam was born in 1891, into the same time and destiny as Nikolai Gumilev, Velimir Khlebnikov, Vladimir Mayakovsky, Sergei Essenin, Marina Tsvetaeva, poets to whom we can apply Roman Jakobson's word that they were 'wasted' by their generation — a word whose implications we have not yet begun to fathom. Mandelstam, to a degree unequalled by his contemporaries, made the poem into a place where all we can perceive and attain through language is gathered around a centre which provides form and truth, around the existence of an individual who challenges the hour, his own and the world's, the heartbeat of the aeon. This is to show how much Mandelstam's poems, risen out of the ruin of a ruined man, are relevant to us today.

In Russia, their land of origin, Mandelstam's volumes (*The Stone*, 1913, *Tristia*, 1922, and *Poems*, 1928, the volume containing the verse written after the October Revolution) are still silenced, non-existent, at best mentioned in passing. A new edition of Mandelstam's poems, as well as of his important stories and essays, appeared in 1955 from Chekhov publishers, New York, with an introduction by Gleb Struve and Boris Filippov-Filistinsky.

What marked the poems most deeply, their profound and tragic agreement with their time, also marked the poet's own path: in the course of Stalin's 'purges', in the nineteen-thirties, he was deported to Siberia. Whether he died there or, as the *Times Literary Supplement* claimed, returned to share the fate of other Jews in those parts of Russia occupied by Hitler's armies, is a question impossible to answer at this point.

The intellectual context of Mandelstam's writing, its Russian, but also Jewish, Greek and Latin heritage, its religious and philosophical thought, is still largely unexplored. (Regarding him, as is commonly done, as one of the 'Acmeists' shows only one aspect of his altogether unusual work.)

This selection in German is the first larger translation in book form; there have only been single poems published in Italian, French and English. I want to give it above all the chance which poetry needs most: the chance simply to exist.

May 9, 1959

Sources

Prose

'Edgar Jené and the Dream about the Dream'
Paul Celan, *Edgar Jené und der Traum vom Traume*. With 30 illustrations and an introduction by Otto Basil. Vienna: Agathon, 1948.
'Backlight'
'Gegenlicht', in *Die Tat*, (Zürich), 12 March 1949.
'Reply to a Questionnaire from the Flinker Bookstore, Paris, 1958' ('Antwort auf eine Umfrage der Librairie Flinker, Paris, 1958'), in *Almanach 1958*, Paris: Les Editions Flinker, 1958, p. 45.
'Conversation in the Mountains'
'Gespräch im Gebirg', in *Die Neue Rundschau*, 71, No. 2 (1960), pp. 199–202.
'Reply to a Questionnaire from the Flinker Bookstore, Paris, 1961'
('Antwort auf eine Umfrage der Librairie

Flinker, Paris, 1961'), in *Almanach 1961*, Paris: Les Editions Flinker, 1961.

'Letter to Hans Bender'
('Brief an Hans Bender'), in Hans Bender, ed., *Mein Gedicht ist mein Messer*, München: List, 1961, p. 86f.
Page 166 carries an editor's note: 'Paul Celan gave permission to publish his letter on the condition that it be published "as such, as a letter written to you today (18 May 1960)".'

'Reply to a Poll by *Der Spiegel*'
('Antwort auf eine *Spiegel*-Umfrage'), in *DER SPIEGEL fragte: Ist eine Revolution unvermeidlich?*, Hamburg: Spiegel-Verlag, 1968. The quote from Hans Magnus Enzensberger is taken from his essay, 'The Writer and Politics' in *The Times Literary Supplement* (London), 28 September 1967, p. 857f.

La poésie ne s'impose plus, elle s'expose.
Single sentence printed, with the date of 26 March 1969, in *L'Ephémère* (Paris), No. 14 (1970), p. 184.

Speeches

'Speech on the Occasion of Receiving the Literature Prize of the Free Hanseatic City of Bremen'
'Ansprache anlässlich der Entgegennahme des Literaturpreises der Freien Hansestadt Bremen' [26 January 1958], in *Paul Celan — Ansprachen bei Verleihung des Bremer Literaturpreises an Paul*

Celan, Stuttgart: Deutsche Verlags-Anstalt, 1958.

'The Meridian'

Der Meridian. Rede anlässlich der Verleihung des Georg-Büchner-Preises, Darmstadt, am 22. Oktober 1960. Frankfurt am Main: S. Fischer, 1961.

'Address to the Hebrew Writers' Association' ('Ansprache vor dem hebräischen Schriftsteller-verband'), in *Die Stimme* (Tel Aviv), August 1970, p. 7.